Published by Hachette Partworks Ltd
ISBN: 978-1-906965-50-1
Date of Printing: January 2011
Printed in Singapore by Tien Wah Press

The Sword in the Stone

Disney
hachette

A long time ago, a king of England died. He had no sons, so nobody knew who would be the next king. Then a sword magically appeared in a churchyard in London. The sword was stuck into a stone, and on it was engraved the words:

Who so pulleth out this sword...
Is rightwise King born of England.

All the knights in the land tried to pull out the sword, but not one of them could do it. So everyone forgot about the sword and got on with their lives.

Far away from London there lived a boy named Arthur, but everyone called him Wart. He was the page to a knight called Sir Ector.

One day Wart went hunting with Kay, Sir Ector's son. Kay spotted a deer in the forest and took aim with his bow and arrow.

But before Kay could shoot, Wart fell out of a tree, making Kay miss the deer. Kay angrily sent Wart into the forest to fetch the arrow.

While searching for the arrow, Wart discovered an old man and an owl, living in a strange house.

"I've been expecting you, though I can't remember why," said the man.

When the old man finally remembered, he explained that he was a magician called Merlin and that he was going to be Wart's tutor.

"I do need a tutor," said Wart. "I haven't had one in ages."

"Then I'll come home with you," said Merlin. "Everything, PACK!" he added, waving his wand.

At once, all Merlin's things packed themselves into a small bag!

Merlin and Wart arrived at Sir Ector's castle.

"Where have you been, Wart?" scolded Sir Ector. "And who's that with you?"

Wart explained that Merlin was a magician who was going to be his teacher. Sir Ector didn't believe it.

"You doubt me?" said Merlin. "Watch!"

Suddenly, a fierce snowstorm blew up – inside the room! Sir Ector was convinced.

"You can be Wart's tutor," he said. "But no more snow!"

That night, Sir Ector's friend, Sir Pelinore, brought news from London. There would be a tournament on New Year's Day – and the winner would be crowned King of England! Sir Ector was convinced that Kay would be the victor.

Sir Ector decided that Wart would go to London with Kay.

"You will be Kay's squire," he declared.

The next day, Merlin began Wart's education.
"Aquarius aquaticus aqualitus!" he chanted, waving his wand. Immediately, Wart and Merlin were transformed into fish!
They swam in the castle moat, but then a big, hungry pike spotted Wart.
"Don't panic, use your head!" advised Merlin.
Wart managed to escape the pike's snapping jaws, while Merlin looked on approvingly.

Back at the castle, Sir Ector didn't believe Wart's story about the pike. He gave the boy extra kitchen chores to do, but Merlin worked some magic and the kitchen began to clean itself.

The pair went outside to continue Wart's training. This time, Merlin decided they would be squirrels. As they bounded from branch to branch, Wart met a girl squirrel who seemed very interested in him!

Wart turned to Merlin for help.

"You're on your own, lad," said Merlin. "I'm afraid magic can't solve *this* problem!"

Meanwhile, at the castle, the maid ran to Sir Ector. "The kitchen is bewitched!" she screamed.

Sir Ector and Kay did battle with the magic brooms, dishes, pots and pans. Soon the whole kitchen was strewn with smashed crockery!

Sir Ector was furious. He told Wart that he was no longer Kay's squire, and wouldn't be allowed to go to London, after all!

Wart was very downcast, but Merlin insisted that Wart must carry on with his education.

Archimedes the owl tried to teach Wart the alphabet, but he was much more interested in Merlin's model flying machines.

"I've always dreamed of flying," he said wistfully.

All of a sudden, Merlin waved his wand. Wart was turned into a bird!

Wart was thrilled. He flew off, followed by Archimedes. Soon he was gliding skilfully through the air.

"Boy, you're a natural!" exclaimed the owl.

Suddenly, a huge, hungry hawk swooped down towards them.

Wart flew for his life. He just managed to escape the hawk's clutches by flying down a chimney.

Wart landed with a bump in a fireplace. A strange old woman with purple hair picked him up and glared at him with mean, yellow eyes.

"I'm the magificent, marvellous, mad Madame Mim!' cackled the hideous old woman.

Madame Mim turned herself into a cat and began to chase Wart all through her house.

Wart was terrified!

Luckily, Merlin burst through the door just in time to save Wart's life.

Madame Mim was angry that Merlin had foiled her evil plan. She challenged him to a wizards' duel.

Madame Mim laid down the rules of the duel. They weren't allowed to turn themselves into make-believe creatures, or to disappear.

But Madame Mim was a cheat. She disappeared as soon as Merlin turned his back! Merlin changed into a tiny caterpillar, so Madame Mim became a big, fat hen and tried to peck him.

Merlin changed into a walrus, so Mim became an elephant. Merlin changed into a mouse and Mim turned into a tiger, then a snake.

Then Mim cheated again. She became a purple dragon. But Merlin turned into a germ and gave Madame Mim a streaming cold and a nasty rash!

"You should recover in a few weeks," smiled Merlin.

Back at the castle, the news was that Kay's new squire had caught mumps. Sir Ector decided Wart would go to London after all!

At the tournament, the knights tried to knock each other off their horses. All the lords and ladies watched and cheered!

Kay started to get ready for the fight. But where was his sword?

"Oh no! I left it back at the inn," confessed Wart.

Wart and Archimedes raced back to the inn where they had stayed the night before.

But the door of the inn was locked. Everyone was at the tournament.

"What'll I do?" said Wart desperately.

Just then, he saw something in a nearby churchyard. It was a sword stuck in a stone!

Wart tugged on the sword. It came out easily.

Wart hurried back to the tournament with the sword. When Sir Ector saw the engraved message on the sword, he couldn't believe his eyes.

"It's the Sword in the Stone!" he cried. The crowd gasped and the tournament stopped.

Sir Ector ordered Wart to show him where he had found the sword.

Wart led the way back to the stone, followed by all the lords and knights.

Sir Ector put the sword back in the stone. Kay tried to pull it out, but it wouldn't budge.

Then one by one, all the other knights tried, but the sword was stuck fast.

Finally, Wart stepped forward. He pulled on the sword and it slipped out easily.

"It's a miracle!" exclaimed one of the knights.

"Hail King Arthur!" they all cheered. "Long live the King!"

Arthur was afraid he wasn't worthy to be King, but wise old Merlin reappeared to reassure him.

"You'll become a great legend," he said. "They'll be writing books about you for centuries to come!"

So began the glorious reign of King Arthur. He was a good and noble ruler, and of course Merlin and Archimedes were always on hand to help!